JUNIOR GYMN

How important is winning?

Look inside for a letter from
U.S.A. Olympic Gymnast Dominique Dawes!
She has a special message just for you!

#1 Dana's Competition

BY TEDDY SLATER

SCHOLASTIC

MALLORY

Dear Junior Gymnast:

Hi! I'm Dominique Dawes, and I love gymnastics too. In 1995, I won two gold medals in the U.S. Gymnastics Championships. The year before that, I won five!

I remember my first gymnastics competition. I was nine years old. I went to the competition with my gymnastics team, the Hill's Angels Club in Wheaton, Maryland. My best friend, Cathy, was also in my club. We both really wanted to do our best and win a medal!

I was so scared when they called my name to compete. My knees were shaking! When I walked onto the mats to start my floor routine, I froze. But then I heard my coach, Kelli Hill, cheering me on. I heard Cathy cheering for me, too. I knew then that everything would be okay. I won that competition. Cathy came in second. But what I will remember most about my first competition is not the gold medal, but how my friend and my coach cheered for me when I really needed them.

In this book, Dana Lewis competes in her first gymnastics meet.

I hope you like this book!

Dominique Dawes

Read more books about the Junior Gymnasts!

Dana's Competition

Dana's Competition

BY TEDDY SLATER

illustrated by Wayne Alfano

A
LITTLE APPLE
PAPERBACK

SCHOLASTIC INC.
New York Toronto London Auckland Sydney

With special thanks to
Tom Manganiello of
57th Street Magic Gym.

A PARACHUTE PRESS BOOK

ISBN 0-590-85997-8

Text copyright © 1996 by Parachute Press, Inc.
Illustrations copyright © 1996 by Scholastic Inc.
Inside cover photo © Doug Pensinger/ALLSPORT USA
LITTLE APPLE PAPERBACKS and the LITTLE APPLE PAPERBACKS logo
are registered trademarks of Scholastic Inc.
All rights reserved. Published by Scholastic Inc.

12 11 10 9 8 7 6 5   6 7 8 9/9 0 1/0

Printed in the U.S.A.   40

First Scholastic printing, June 1996

For the real Becky — Becky Margulies
— with love.

Contents

Dana's Competition

Winning Dreams

Thunk! As soon as my feet hit the springboard, I knew it was going to be a good one.

It was a Thursday afternoon at Jody's Gym, and I was about to do my best vault ever. I nailed my handspring off the horse and made a perfect landing!

Coach Jody gave me a thumbs-up sign. "Great job, Dana," she said. "If you do it that way at the meet next Saturday, I guarantee you'll come home with a medal."

"A gold one?" I asked, crossing my fingers for luck.

"I wouldn't be surprised," she answered.

I'm Dana. Dana Lewis. And I'm on Coach Jody's Level 5 Gymnastics Team. I've been doing gymnastics ever since my mother signed me up for Teeter Tots when I was three.

I'm nine now. Being a Level 5 gymnast means I start competing this year! My very first gymnastics meet will be a week from Saturday. My whole team has been practicing for ages. I can hardly wait!

My fingers were still crossed when Coach Jody said, "Come on, Dana. We're not through yet. Let's see you do that again."

Coach Jody is Jody James. She's the best gymnastics coach in the world. The tallest, too, I bet. Six foot one! If it wasn't for that, she could have been in the Olympics. But gymnasts have to be small. It has something to do with your center of gravity.

Coach Jody says her Olympic dreams ended when she was twelve — because she broke a hand and grew a foot! Actually, she grew only four inches, but it was enough to keep her from competing.

I'm sorry Coach Jody didn't get to be in the Olympics. But I'm happy she's a coach, because someday *I'm* going to be an Olympic champion! And I need Coach Jody to teach me how.

My whole team wants to be in the Olympics. We work with Coach Jody three times a week — Mondays, Wednesdays, and Thursdays. And we work *hard*.

Besides me, Hannah Rose Crenshaw is the best gymnast on the team. She's also the bossiest. The other girls are Liz Halsey, Emily Stone, and Katie Magee. Except for Katie, we're all in the fourth grade at Lincoln Elementary School.

Katie is my best friend on the team. She's in third grade, and she goes to

Washington Elementary. All the schools in Springfield are named after dead presidents! Don't ask me why.

"I'll race you!" I told Katie after practice. I sat on my bicycle, waiting for her.

She jumped on her bike and pedaled after me. By the time we reached the corner of Cranberry and Sixth, I was out of breath. I stopped under the big oak tree on the corner. We call it the Good-bye Tree, because that's where we say good-bye!

"No fair!" cried Katie as she rode up behind me. "You had a head start!" She was laughing.

I climbed off my bike and did a handstand on the grass near the tree. My hair fell over my eyes, so I had to peek between the curls to see Katie. I crossed my eyes.

Katie giggled.

"Hey, Katie?" I asked. "Do you think I'll win a medal on vault?"

"Definitely!" Katie said. "I bet you win one on bars, too."

I didn't want to sound stuck-up, so I said, "I wish!" But actually, I felt sure I could do it. Besides the vault, my favorite event is the uneven parallel bars.

I took a few steps on my hands. Then I put my feet down and stood up straight.

Katie took the scrunchie out of her ponytail, and her long blond hair fell across her face. "I wonder if *I'll* win anything," she said softly. I could hardly hear her.

"You will!" I said. "There are four events. And they give three medals for each event. That's twelve chances."

"I'd be happy with one!" Katie said.

We talked about the meet until it started getting dark. Then Katie said, "I'd better go now. I have a math test tomorrow, and I have to study."

"You're great at math. You'll get a

hundred," I said. I climbed back on my bike.

Then Katie turned left and I turned right. "Bye!" we both yelled as we pedaled away. That's how the Good-bye Tree works.

When I got home, Becky Berkman was in the kitchen with my mom. Katie is my best friend in gymnastics, and Becky is my best best friend in the whole world. We were born just one week apart — and we've been friends ever since!

"Hi, Beck!" I said. I dumped my books and gym bag on the counter. "What's up?"

"I need spelling help," Becky said. "We have a quiz tomorrow, remember?"

"Okay," I said. "Mom, can Becky stay for dinner?"

"Of course," answered Mom. "We're having ravioli."

Becky grinned. She loves my mom's ravioli.

"Dinner's almost ready. Will you get your brother?" Mom asked. "He's in the den."

I almost tripped over Woof on my way into the den. Woof is supposed to be *my* dog. But lately she's been hanging out with my brother Freddy a lot. I guess that's because I'm always in school or at the gym. Freddy is only four, so he never goes anywhere.

"I didn't do it," Freddy said. He pointed to a big vase on the floor. Flowers and leafy water dripped all over the rug.

"*She* did it!" Freddy added as Woof slurped up the water.

I laughed. I never get mad at Freddy — no matter how much of a mess he makes. Becky says I like Freddy because he's a younger version of me. He has red hair, big green eyes, and freckles, just like I do!

I grabbed some paper towels and

cleaned up the mess. Then it was time for dinner.

"Hi, Daddy," I said, running into the dining room. I sat down next to Becky and reached for the bread. I'm always extra-hungry on gym days. Dad passed the salad to me.

"Becky was just telling us about her karate lessons," said Mom.

"I'm going to break bricks with my bare hands!" Becky announced.

"When did you start karate?" I asked.

"I didn't start yet," Becky admitted. "My mom wants me to take ballet. She says I'm wild enough as it is."

Becky started gymnastics when I did. But she got bored with it after a year. Then she tried juggling, then figure skating, then the trumpet, then Little League, and finally tap dancing. Becky was bored with everything.

"Speaking of lessons," Dad said. "How was gym today?"

"Great," I answered. "I did a super vault. I kept my toes pointed and my legs together and everything. Coach Jody says I'll win a medal at the meet for sure. Katie thinks I'll win two."

"Why stop at two?" Dad asked with a smile.

"Maybe I won't," I said. "Maybe I'll win three. Or even — "

"Hey, slow down, honey," Dad interrupted. "I was only kidding. Your mother and I don't care how many medals you win."

"Well, I care how many I win," I said. "And I'm going to win a lot. Just wait and see!"

The New Girl

The Teeter Tots class was just ending when I got to the gym on Monday. The little girls laughed and screamed as they ran through the locker room.

I saw Emily, Liz, and Hannah Rose crowded into one corner of the locker room. A little girl in silver sneakers was jumping up and down on Hannah Rose's gym bag. Hannah Rose gave her a dirty look. She doesn't like the Teeter Tots.

"Hi, Katie!" I called. I dropped my gym bag onto the bench and unzipped it. "What are you writing?"

"I'm writing about what happened in school today," she answered. Katie was already dressed for practice. She sat on the floor, scribbling in the notebook she carries everywhere.

I pulled my leotard from my gym bag. I was just wiggling into it when a girl I had never seen before walked in. She looked about my age.

"Katie!" I whispered. "Who is that?"

Katie glanced up and frowned. "I don't know. She must be new."

Hannah Rose came over to us. "Look at that new girl!" she said. "She's wearing all pink!"

The new girl wore a pink shirt, a pink pleated skirt, and matching pink socks. Her skin was a beautiful coppery-brown color. She had long black hair, and long, long legs, and the most perfect posture. She looked more like a ballerina than a gymnast.

"Should we say hello?" Katie asked.

The all-pink girl took one look around the locker room and headed for the far corner. She put her pink gym bag down on the bench and began getting undressed.

"Even her underwear is pink!" Hannah Rose said. She giggled.

The new girl folded her skirt slowly and neatly. Then she took off her pink shirt and folded it just as carefully. She tucked her pink socks into her pink shoes and lined them up under the bench. And finally, she took a pink leotard out of her bag and stepped into it.

By the time she was done, the little kids were gone. I was still standing there with my basic black leotard around my knees.

"What's taking you so long, Dana?" Katie asked. She, Emily, Liz, and Hannah

Rose were dressed and ready to go. I suddenly noticed that their leotards were all kind of faded.

I glanced down at my own leotard. It was kind of a splotchy gray from being washed so many times.

"You'd better hurry, Dana," Hannah Rose said in her bossy voice. "Coach Jody doesn't like it when we're late."

I pulled my leotard up and tossed my school clothes into my locker. "Maybe we should get new leos," I whispered to Katie as we walked out of the locker room. "Mine is at least a year old!"

Katie looked at me as if I were crazy. "I have an extra one in my gym bag if you want it," she offered.

"No, I just mean . . . well, our leos don't look very nice." I usually don't care how my leotard looks. But that all-pink girl made me feel sloppy.

The new girl was stretching in front of

a mirror in the gym. She held one long leg straight up over her head with one hand. Even her toenails were polished pink!

Coach Jody was waiting for us at the front of the gym. "Take your places, girls," she said. "There's someone I want you to meet."

She called the new girl over and said, "Everyone say hello to Amanda Calloway!"

The girl didn't smile. But she didn't look scared, either. She just gazed at us with big brown eyes.

"The Calloways just moved to Springfield," Coach Jody said. "And we're lucky they did! Amanda has been competing for almost a year. She won two medals in her last competition. Amanda was the star of her old team, and I'm sure she is going to shine on this team, too. So let's give our new star a warm welcome!"

Everyone clapped, so I did, too. But

my stomach lurched. I thought *I* was supposed to be the star of our team!

"Okay," Coach Jody said. "Now that our hands are warmed up, let's get those bodies moving. It's warm-up time! Let's go."

We always start warm-up by jogging around the gym a few times. Then we run faster. That's to get our heart rates up. Then we add arm movements. Sometimes we flap our arms up and down like wings. Sometimes we wave them in the air like maniacs. I like the maniac way best.

After twenty minutes of running, jumping, and stretching, I was soaked in sweat. Everyone else looked pretty soggy, too. Everyone except Amanda Calloway.

"Now let's get to work," Coach Jody said. "We have only three more sessions before the meet on Saturday. I want you all to make the most of them."

Coach Jody led us over to the balance beam. "Today I want to try something different," she said. "Instead of doing a little bit of everything, we'll be working just on beam."

I took a step forward. I *always* go first.

"Amanda, let's start with you," added Coach Jody.

I stopped, surprised. Everyone turned to stare at Amanda. But she was gazing straight ahead at the beam.

"Are you ready, Amanda?" Coach Jody asked.

Amanda nodded without taking her eyes off the beam. Then she ran forward and did a perfect squat mount.

Usually, when Coach Jody works with someone, the rest of us go off and practice our balancing skills. But this time, we all just stood around and watched the new girl.

Amanda Calloway went through the whole Level 5 routine without one little wobble. It was the same routine we all practiced. The same one we would do at the

17

meet. But it didn't look the same. It looked better. A lot better!

Amanda didn't stumble, or lean, or slip. She made the beam routine look easy. Her dismount was as good as her mount. She really nailed the landing. Then she straightened her knees, threw out her arms, and smiled a huge smile.

Coach Jody is always reminding us to finish our routines with a smile. Even if we've just done horribly and feel more like crying. But Amanda didn't need to be reminded.

There was a moment of silence. Then everybody clapped.

"That looked terrific," Coach Jody exclaimed. "Now let's see what the rest of you can do."

We all lined up. Katie fell off the beam twice and Emily was a little shaky on her turns. My routine went pretty well. But it didn't come close to Amanda's.

We finished the practice with our usual strength exercises and cool-down. Then Coach Jody said, "That's it for today, girls. See you all on Wednesday."

The coach called Amanda over to sign some forms while the rest of us headed to our lockers. As soon as we reached the locker room, everyone started talking about Amanda and how great she was.

Katie was still talking about her as we got on our bikes. She talked about her till we came to the Good-bye Tree. But Katie wasn't ready to say good-bye yet.

"I can't believe Amanda Calloway is on our team," Katie said. "She seems a lot better than Level 5. Did you see how she kept her toes pointed during her whole routine? She was great! I wish I could be like Amanda Calloway. Don't you?"

I didn't know what to say. First of all, I thought I *was* like Amanda — a great gymnast. And second, I didn't like the way

Katie kept using her whole name. Amanda Calloway! It made her sound like a movie star or something.

"Why don't you just call her Amanda?" I asked. "It's not as if there are two Amandas on our team."

"I wish there were," Katie said. "Then we would definitely win the competition on Saturday! I think Amanda Calloway is just what we need!"

"Maybe," I said. "But I think one Amanda is enough. More than enough!"

★ 3

A Too Blue Day

Amanda Calloway showed up for the next practice all in blue. Blue denim overalls. A blue tie-dyed T-shirt. And blue suede sneakers. This time I didn't even blink when she put her dark blue leotard over her light blue underwear.

"Today we're going to work on the vault and uneven bars," Coach Jody said as soon as we finished our warm-up.

Good! I thought. My two best events!

Amanda went first. Her handspring off the vault was huge! She practically flew over the horse.

Everybody oohed and aahed. But at least they didn't applaud.

"That's what I call a vault!" Coach Jody said. "I'm getting a very good feeling about Saturday's meet," she added. "I think our team is going to do very, very well there."

And then everybody *did* applaud.

"Okay, Dana, you're up next," Coach Jody called.

I ran toward the horse. I could feel Amanda's eyes on me. I'll show her, I thought. *I'm* the one who will win the vault on Saturday!

But somehow I didn't get enough height on my takeoff. My handstand on the horse wobbled, and I couldn't keep my legs together on the dismount. When I landed, I smiled the way we're supposed to. But nobody applauded for me. Nobody was even watching! Except Coach Jody. And Amanda Calloway.

Amanda's routine on the uneven bars looked just as good as her vault. It was hard to tell where one move ended and the other began. That's how smooth she looked.

This time Coach Jody didn't say anything. She just shook her head and grinned. Practice seemed to drag on and on. Every time I tried a move, I saw Amanda watching me. She made me so nervous! When I did my routine on the bars, I actually fell off in the middle!

For once, I was glad when Coach Jody said, "That's it for today." I couldn't take one more minute of Amanda the Perfect!

I hurried into the locker room and took a quick shower. Then I changed back into my school clothes. I looked for Katie. She was standing *inside* her locker!

"Come on, Katie," I said. "I have to get home early. I promised Mom I would take care of Freddy today."

Mom used to work at a sewing magazine called *Pins and Needles*. She left that job when I was born, but she still writes some articles at home. She needs quiet when she works, so I watch Freddy for her.

"I can't leave," Katie said. "I lost my pencil case."

"What does it look like?" Amanda asked.

"Like a red rubber shark with yellow fins," Hannah Rose chimed in. "It has big silver zipper teeth that open up so you can put stuff in it."

"It's a *fat* red rubber shark," I added. Katie keeps about a million pencils in her pencil case. She needs them. When she isn't writing in her journal, she's writing letters. She has fourteen pen pals in eleven different countries.

"Did you check your gym bag?" I asked.

"I already looked," Katie answered. "But I guess I should check again."

She opened her bag and pulled out: a smelly black leotard, a clean white towel, an empty water bottle, a small first-aid kit, a roll of gymnastics tape, a plastic jar of hand cream, two sets of bar grips, and one sock. She peered into the bag, which was still stuffed! Katie pushed aside a giant bag of Gummi Bears and said, "I still don't see the pencil case! Where could it be?"

Everyone joined in the search. We looked under the benches and on top of them. We checked out the showers and the toilet stalls. But no pencil case.

I looked up at the clock and groaned. It was getting late.

Katie looked at the clock too. "Maybe you should go without me," she said.

"Well . . ." I didn't want to leave Katie. But my mom was waiting for me.

"Don't worry, Katie," Amanda said. "I'll help you look."

"Great!" said Katie.

I turned to Katie. "Are you sure?" I asked.

"Sure," Katie and Amanda said together. Then they both laughed.

"Well . . ." I said again. But Katie and Amanda were already emptying out Katie's locker. They were still laughing. I wasn't sure if Katie heard me. But she didn't seem to care if I left. I walked down the front steps and unlocked my bike. Then I rode away. Alone.

It's bad enough that Amanda Calloway is a better gymnast than me, I thought. Does she have to become better friends with Katie, too?

4

Telephone Talk

When I got home, my mother gave me a hug. "Hi, sweetie," she said. "Thanks for coming straight home. I really need to get some work done." She went into the spare room and closed the door.

When the door is open, we call that room our den. But when Mom shuts the door, it becomes her office. No one is even supposed to knock unless it's an emergency.

As soon as Mom turned on the computer, Freddy grabbed Woof's favorite squeaky toy. They began to play fetch. I made myself a snack. Then I sat at the kitchen table so I could keep an eye on Freddy. I picked up the phone and called Katie.

Her phone rang twice. Then the answering machine picked up:

"To hear from Pat or Katie Mageeee,
Just leave a message at the beeee-p!"

The voice on the machine was Mrs. Magee's — except for the "p" sound. That was definitely Katie's. So was the giggle that followed it.

I giggled, too. "Hi, Katie!" I said. "It's me. Cool message. Call me when you get home. 'Bye."

The Magees used to have a regular boring phone message. But then Mr. and Mrs. Magee got divorced. Now Katie's mom likes to have a new funny message every day. At first, she made Katie record them with her. But Katie hated that. So now Katie makes up the messages, and her mother says them.

I looked at the clock on my desk. It was 5:42. Where *was* Katie, anyway?

Katie called back at eight o'clock. "Sorry I didn't call sooner," she said. "Mom made me wait till we finished eating."

"Where were you when I called?" I asked.

"You're not going to believe this. . . ." Katie paused dramatically. "But I was at Amanda Calloway's house!"

"Amanda's?" I repeated. "How come you went there?"

"Well, after you left, I still couldn't find my pencil case. I looked all over. Guess what? It was in my gym bag all along!"

"I'm glad you found your pencil case," I told her. "But what does that have to do with Amanda?"

"Everything," Katie said. "By the time

I found it, we were the only ones still in the locker room. So we left together. And it turns out she lives on Cranberry Street — just a block away from me! She's been there for three whole weeks, and I never even saw her. She goes to Washington Elementary with me. Isn't that amazing?"

"Amazing," I said.

"Anyway," Katie went on, "when we got to her house, she invited me in. So I went."

"Then what?" I asked.

"Well, she lives in this humongous house with her mother, her father, her grandmother, and two sisters and a brother," Katie began. "Isn't that cool?"

I guess it sounded cool to Katie because she's an only child. It seemed like a lot of people to me.

But Katie didn't wait for my answer. "Amanda's closet is as big as my whole room," she said. "And all her clothes are lined up by color. The pink things are on the left side. Then come the red ones, and then the green . . . I don't remember the rest of them. Amanda only wears one color at a time. Tomorrow is her yellow day. She says it's lucky to wear just one color a day. She says that's why she always wins in gymnastics — because she wears her lucky colors!"

"Well, I hope she doesn't really believe that," I said. "There's more to winning than luck. I'm as good as she is — maybe *I'll* win."

Katie was quiet for a second. "I don't think she meant it that way," she said. She sounded surprised. "Amanda is really nice. I think she just likes to be lucky."

"I guess," I said. But I thought Amanda sounded stuck-up.

"Anyway," Katie went on. "Everyone in Amanda's family has their own pet. Amanda has a Great Dane puppy. Her big sister has two parrots that talk to each

other. Her little sister has a kitten. And her brother has two rabbits with ears that go down instead of up. They're a special kind."

I could tell Katie was excited. She loves animals more than anything. She wants to be a veterinarian when she grows up. But her mom is allergic to anything with fur or feathers. So the only pets Katie can ever have are fish and reptiles.

"Even Amanda's grandmother has a pet," Katie went on. "A ferret named Farfel! He — "

Katie's voice broke off at the sound of the call-waiting click. "Hold on a minute," she said.

I waited a lot more than a minute. In fact, I was about to hang up when Katie came back on the line.

"Dana, it's Amanda! 'Bye," Katie said all in a rush. And then she hung up on me!

I was still staring at the phone when it rang again.

"Hi, Katie," I said. "We must have gotten disconnect — "

"HAiii-*yaaa!*" someone screamed in my ear.

"Katie?" I said.

"Of course not," a familiar voice replied. "It's me."

"Oh, hi, Becky," I said. "Why are you screaming?"

"That was my karate yell," Becky explained. "My mom said if I don't do anything annoying for the rest of the week, she'll let me take lessons. Isn't that great?"

"Yeah," I said. "It really is, Beck."

"Are you okay?" Becky asked.

"Yeah," I said. "It's just that there's this new girl in gymnastics. Amanda Calloway. She's such a show-off! She thinks she's the best gymnast in the world. Coach Jody thinks she's great. And so does Katie. I bet she and Amanda will be best friends."

"So what?" Becky said. "I'm *your* best

friend. And I think *you* are the best gymnast in the world."

"Thanks," I said. "But Amanda's already won about a million medals."

"Big deal," Becky said. "I bet you'll win a million and one at the meet on Saturday. You've always been the best gymnast on your team. Coach Jody knows that. And after Saturday, Amanda-the-Show-Off Calloway will know it, too."

"You're right, Becky," I said. "I'll show Amanda that she's not so hot. And I may not wait till Saturday, either."

5
Showing Off

Even though Katie warned me, I still did a double take when Amanda showed up on Thursday. She was dressed all in yellow.

Coach Jody smiled when she walked into the gym. "Amanda," she said. "You look just like a ray of sunshine!"

"She looks more like a big banana," I muttered.

"Did you say something, Dana?" Coach Jody asked.

"No," I answered quickly.

"All right," Coach Jody called. "Before we get started, I want to talk about the competition on Saturday. I know you've all seen lots of local meets. Amanda has even competed in some. But every — "

"I won two medals," Amanda broke in.

"That's great, Amanda," Coach Jody said with a smile. "But as I was saying, every meet is different. If you know what to expect, you won't be too nervous on Saturday."

I glanced around at the other girls. They looked nervous already. All of a sudden, I felt nervous, too. My first competition was only two days away!

"You all know your routines," Coach Jody said. "But there will be a lot happening on Saturday. You'll be doing your beam routine while someone else is doing her vault. The audience may cheer when she finishes — even if you're right in the middle of your handstand. So it's very important to concentrate on what you're doing. That means shutting out everything else."

I decided to practice by shutting out everything but the sound of Coach Jody's voice. It wasn't easy. Katie was scratching her arm. Hannah Rose and Emily were giggling about something. Liz cracked her knuckles. Amanda was the only one who didn't make a sound. She stared at Coach Jody. I wondered if she was shutting out everything else, too.

"There will be three other teams at the meet," Coach Jody explained. "The winners in each event will get a medal — gold for first place, silver for second, and bronze for third."

Out of the corner of my eye, I saw Amanda smile when Coach Jody said "gold."

"And best of all," Coach Jody continued, "the team with the highest total of points wins a silver cup."

"Do we get to keep the cup?" Emily wanted to know.

"You bet," Coach Jody said. "At least for a year," she added. "Then we have to compete for it again. But let's not get ahead of ourselves. First things first. Which reminds me . . ."

Coach Jody's voice trailed off as she picked up a big white box that was on the floor behind her.

"These are for Saturday," she said. "Your official team uniforms!" She pulled out a leotard and held it up for us to see. Everybody gasped. The leotards were beautiful. They were bright red with big gold stars on the front.

Coach Jody handed one to each of us. I stared at mine. My very first gymnastics uniform. For my very first competition. *I'll be wearing this when I win my first gold medal!* I thought happily.

"These are *soooo* cool," Katie said.

"They look just like the ones in the Olympics," Liz agreed.

Hannah Rose held hers up to her shoulders. "I love mine!"

"I can't wear this on Saturday," Amanda said.

Everyone stopped talking. Everyone stared at Amanda.

"Why not?" Hannah Rose asked.

"I always wear lavender on Saturday," Amanda said, as if that explained it.

"Well, I'm afraid you'll have to make an exception this time," Coach Jody told her. "You all have to wear matching uniforms — you're a team! Wait until you try it on, Amanda. I'm sure you'll love it."

"That isn't the problem," Amanda said.

"Then what is?" Coach Jody asked.

"Lavender is my lucky Saturday color," Amanda explained. "If I don't wear my lavender leotard, I won't win any gold medals."

Coach Jody looked a little confused. I didn't blame her. I couldn't believe how stuck-up Amanda was! What made her so sure she'd win even *with* her lucky leotard?

I tried to catch Katie's eye. But she was watching Amanda.

"I have an idea," said Coach Jody. "If lavender is your lucky color, why don't you wear something lavender with the leotard?"

"Like what?" Amanda asked.

"You could wear a lavender wrist-band," Liz suggested. "Or maybe lavender underwear."

"How about lavender nail polish?" Emily said.

Amanda didn't say a word. She just shook her head "No" at every suggestion.

"I could make you a lavender friendship bracelet," Katie offered.

Finally Amanda spoke up. She sounded really upset. "Everything is supposed to be the same color." Her voice trembled. "That's why it's lucky."

"I know," Katie said. "But wouldn't a

little bit of lavender be better than none?"

"I guess," Amanda admitted.

"I'm sure you'll work it out," Coach Jody said. "In the meantime, let's get to work. This is our last chance before the meet to polish up those floor exercises."

After warm-up, Coach Jody led us to the mats. "Katie, let's start with you for a change," she called.

Katie walked slowly over to the mat. Her face was bright pink. She always likes to go last.

As soon as Katie began her routine, Liz started doing leg lifts. Emily and Hannah Rose went to the beam. We always have to work with a partner when we use the equipment. While one girl practices, the other stands by in case anything goes wrong. It's called spotting.

That left me with Amanda. I didn't want to spot for her. But she didn't even look at me. She just plopped right down on the floor and began doing splits.

First she did a side split with her left leg in front. It looked pretty good. Then she did one with her right leg in front. It looked very good.

I tried a front split. That's harder than a side split. Mine was okay, but not great. I could feel Amanda watching me, so I tried it again. *Much* better. There was hardly any space between me and the floor.

I looked over at Amanda. She was still watching me. I kind of thought she might say something. Like "Wow" or "Good going." But she just kept staring. Finally Amanda spoke up.

"You're not doing it right," she said. "Try it like this." Then she did a totally perfect split. There was no space at all between her and the floor!

I couldn't believe Amanda was such a show-off! "Can you do this?" I asked. I jumped up, did a handstand, and let my legs open up into a split — as far as I could.

Amanda stared at me. Then she kicked up into her own handstand. As she was about to do her split, the whole room got quiet.

"What are you girls doing?" Coach Jody asked.

Amanda and I both jumped to our feet.

"Well?" Coach Jody said.

"Uh, we were having a split contest," I explained.

"To see who could do them better," Amanda added.

Coach Jody sighed. "Uh-oh," she said. "I think all my talk about medals and cups has given you the wrong idea."

Coach Jody put one hand on Amanda's shoulder and one hand on mine. "Listen," she said. "This is a team! We don't compete against one another. If one of you does well, everyone does well. Understand?"

"Yes, Coach Jody," Amanda said quietly.

"Yes, Coach Jody," I added.

"Good," said Coach Jody. "I don't want to see you girls competing with each other. Not in my gym."

Coach Jody turned back to the mats. I glanced at Amanda. She looked back at me. "She didn't say anything about outside," I whispered.

"Outside?" Amanda asked.

"Right. Meet me at the ballfield after practice," I said. "We can finish our competition there."

Amanda smiled. "You're on!"

★ 6
Flipping Out

After practice, we went straight to the baseball diamond. A bunch of older boys were tossing a ball around the outfield. There were some girls sitting in the bleachers. They all had books in their laps. But they weren't reading. They were watching those boys.

Amanda and I marched over to home plate. The rest of our team was right behind us. Nobody said anything.

I stared at Amanda. Amanda glanced at the ground. She looked sort of embarrassed. Suddenly I felt embarrassed, too — I had never challenged anyone to a contest before. I didn't know what to say or do. It's a good thing Hannah Rose was there. She loves telling people what to do.

"Well, are you going to stand here all day?" Hannah Rose demanded. "Amanda, you never finished your handstand split. Do one now."

"I don't want to," Amanda said quietly.

"Don't want to?" I asked. "Or *can't*?"

Amanda looked angry. "I can do a handstand split," she said. "And I can do it better than you." She smoothed down her yellow skirt. "I just can't do it in this," she added. "My skirt will go over my head."

"So what?" I said. "Nobody will see. You're wearing leggings." And she was. Bright yellow ones.

Amanda handed her gym bag to Katie. "Can you hold this for me?" she asked. "Don't let it get dirty." Then she put her hands down on the ground and kicked up her heels.

Amanda was right about the skirt. The minute she was upside down, it flopped over her head. It looked pretty funny. But nobody laughed. They were too busy admiring her split. Amanda was right about that split, too. It was much better than mine.

"Well?" Amanda said when she finished. "Now what?"

"Do a front walkover," Hannah Rose told her.

"That's too easy," Amanda said. And to prove it, she put her arms up, reached forward, and touched both hands to the ground at once. Then she kicked her legs up and over — first the right one and then the left — till she was standing again.

"Much too easy," I agreed. I did a *back* walkover.

"Wow!" someone yelled. "Look at that!"

"Do it again!" someone else yelled.

I turned to see who was making all the noise. It was the girls in the bleachers. They had stopped watching the boys. Now they were watching us. Amanda smiled at the girls and quickly did two back walkovers.

"Awesome!" a boy's voice called out.

The boys in the outfield moved up to first base. They were watching us, too. So were a bunch of little kids standing outside the fence.

"Can you do a tumble sauce?" one of the little kids asked.

"He means a somersault," another kid said.

"A forward roll?" I said. "Of course I can do that!" I did five in a row.

"Cool," the first kid said. "Do more."

"No," Hannah Rose said. "This is getting boring. How about some cartwheels?"

"Okay," I answered. But just as I placed

my hand on the ground, Amanda said "Okay," too. Then she put her hand down.

Before Amanda could finish her first cartwheel, I was already starting my second. And then I was doing my third.

Amanda stayed with me as I cartwheeled down the first-base line. *Four, five, six.* I was counting them in my head when I suddenly heard Hannah Rose's voice:

"Seven . . . eight . . . nine . . ."

Out of the corner of my eye I could see Katie running along beside us. She was screaming, "Dana! Amanda! Stop it! You'll break your arms! You'll break your legs! Please stop!"

But I wasn't about to stop. And neither was Amanda. We both slowed down when we reached first base. I heard Amanda laugh as we changed direction and headed for second.

"You guys," Katie tried again. "You're going to break your heads! The meet is only

two days away. If something happens, you won't even get to — "

But Katie's voice was drowned out by the crowd counting: "Fourteen . . . fifteen . . . sixteen . . ."

When we reached twenty, we stopped. The crowd clapped and yelled. I wasn't dizzy at all. This was fun!

"Let's go for third base," I said to Amanda.

She grinned. "Let's go all the way home!"

We did our first cartwheel together. Then another one. I saw third base about ten feet away.

I'm flying, I thought. Nothing can stop me! I put my hand down for the next cartwheel. And I felt a soft spot in the grass. I caught my breath.

SPLAT! I was flat on my back in a puddle of mud.

The crowd of kids gasped. As soon as I sat up, I heard a giggle. It was Hannah Rose. She quickly put her hand over her mouth. But it was too late.

Someone in the bleachers started to giggle. And then more kids. Soon everyone was laughing out loud. I glanced down at myself. Then I started to giggle, too. I looked like a mud monster!

"Dana, are you all right?" a worried voice asked. Katie hugged me. "I can't believe you fell," she cried. "You shouldn't have tried to keep up with Amanda."

Amanda! I looked around the field and spotted her near home base. She was still cartwheeling! She hadn't even stopped to see if I was hurt.

When she reached home plate, Amanda hopped to her feet and grinned at the crowd. They finally stopped laughing at me — and started cheering for her!

Amanda took a deep bow, and the cheers grew louder. She took another bow.

I climbed to my feet as Amanda came running over. "That was fun!" she said. She grinned at me.

"Not for me," I said.

Amanda looked surprised, but she didn't say anything. Slowly she took her bag from Katie. "Thanks for holding this," she said. "I'll see you at school tomorrow."

Katie nodded.

Then Amanda turned to me. "Sorry about the mud," she said. But she didn't sound sorry.

I stared hard at Amanda. "I'll see you at the meet on Saturday!" I told her.

The Big Day

I thought Saturday would never come. Thursday night and Friday went by in slow motion. All I could think about was my first competition. And about how I could beat Amanda Calloway.

It was still dark when I woke up Saturday morning. I looked at the clock on my desk. It was only five o'clock. I pulled the covers over my head and closed my eyes. But I was too excited to go back to sleep.

I kept my eyes closed and ran through my routines in my mind. I did them all perfectly! The crowd cheered for me. Coach Jody gave me a hug and said I was her best gymnast ever. I won four gold medals.

Then I sat up in bed.

That's the way my first competition will be, I thought. Unless Amanda Calloway ruins everything!

Katie's mother dropped us off at the Riverdale Gym. The competition was starting at eleven o'clock, but all the athletes had to be there by nine A.M.

"Good luck, girls," Mrs. Magee said as we climbed out of the car. "I'll be back in a couple of hours."

Katie looked worried. "Don't be late," she said.

Mrs. Magee hugged Katie. "I won't," she promised.

"C'mon, Katie," I said. "Let's go!"

We checked in and looked for our teammates. They were easy to find! Everyone wore the bright-red team leotard. Even Amanda. But I could see a sparkly lavender barrette in her hair.

"Dana! Katie! Come on," Coach Jody called. "Warm-up starts in five minutes. I want to go over the lineup before we begin."

Coach Jody opened her notebook. "Emily will go first," she said. "Then Liz, Hannah Rose, Katie, Dana, and Amanda. You'll be performing all four events in that order. So please pay attention and make sure you're ready when your turn comes."

Suddenly the PA system crackled. "General warm-ups will now begin," an official-sounding voice announced.

We had twenty minutes to practice each event. Nothing felt the way it did at Jody's Gym. The floor mats were bouncier. The balance beam was harder. The horse was softer. I tried not to think about any of that. I told myself I would be fine if I concentrated on my routines.

I must have been concentrating really hard because I jumped when the loudspeaker blared again: "Warm-ups are now over. There will be a half-hour break before the meet begins."

The gym was packed! As we all marched in, I looked for my family in the crowd. They were right in the first row. Becky and her parents were next to my mom. And Mrs. Magee was next to them.

The Riverdale Middle School chorus sang *The Star-Spangled Banner*. Then the announcer introduced the teams. And then the meet started.

A girl from Central began her floor routine. A Riverdale girl ran toward the horse. Someone from Team Twist mounted the beam. And Emily swung onto the low bar.

I was nervous just watching Emily. This was really scary. Emily scored a 7.1. Liz and Hannah Rose were next. But they must have been nervous, too. They didn't do much better than Emily.

I was so scared that I didn't even want to watch Katie's routine. But she didn't seem nervous at all. Her routine looked great! It wasn't fair that she got only an 8. Coach Jody said it was because she hesitated between moves and didn't always keep her legs together.

Then it was my turn. The first event of my first competition! As I stood in front of the bars, my heart was pounding. I tried to remember the routine. But my mind was a total blank.

The announcer read out my name. "Dana Lewis, Jody's Gym."

I took a deep breath and grabbed the low bar. Suddenly I was straddling the bar just the way I always do. I reached for the high bar. And then I was swinging through the air. I wasn't nervous anymore. I was flying. I came back to earth with a perfect landing!

The crowd went wild. They were still cheering when my score flashed onto the board. A 9.3!

I couldn't stop grinning as I hurried back to our bench. Everyone jumped up and hugged me. Everyone except Amanda. She didn't even look at me! She was staring at the bars. Amanda stood up and walked toward them. Then she did her routine — and Amanda scored a 9.4! She beat me by a tenth of a point!

When Amanda came back to the bench, she smiled at me. But I didn't smile back. I was already thinking about the next event. No matter what, I was going to beat Amanda. I had to show her that I was the star of the team!

★ ★ ★

By the time we reached the balance beam, Amanda and I were tied. I had one gold medal for vault. Amanda had one for bars. Neither of us did well on the floor exercise. The beam was the last event. And only one of us could win the gold medal.

I watched my teammates on the beam. Emily, Liz, and Hannah Rose all made big mistakes. Liz almost fell off the beam! I couldn't believe it. Their scores were terrible.

Katie was next. I was thinking hard about my own routine, so I didn't watch her. Then I heard cheering. I glanced up, and there was Katie in the middle of a super handstand. Her toes were pointed. Her legs were together. And she held the handstand for a really long time. The rest of her routine was amazing! It was the best ever! As soon as we saw her score, our whole team jumped up from the bench. A 9.0!

"Katie, you were awesome!" I cried. "You're in first place!"

Katie's face turned pink. "Just for now," she said. "You and Amanda haven't gone yet. You'll both do better."

"But even if we both got tens, the worst you can do is third," I told her. "All the other teams have lower scores. There's no way you won't win a medal!"

Katie's face turned even pinker. "Is that really true?" she cried. "I can't believe it!"

"Believe it!" Coach Jody said, giving Katie a hug. Then she hugged me, too. "You're next, Dana," she said.

I walked to the beam. I could think of only one thing. To beat Amanda, I would have to do my very, very best!

For the first part of my routine, I concentrated hard. This was my last chance to show Amanda who was the best gymnast! I imagined winning my second gold medal. It was all I could think about. Then I wobbled on my handstand. I barely kept my balance! After that, all my moves were shaky.

The crowd cheered when I finished my dismount. Becky even gave a loud karate yell. But *I* knew I had blown it. I threw out my arms and smiled the way Coach Jody taught us. Then I checked out my score: 9.1. I quickly ducked my head to hide my tears. There was no way I would beat Amanda now.

I kept my head down as I walked to the bench. I was almost there when I spotted a flash of lavender on the bright red mats.

Without stopping, I bent down and picked it up. Amanda's lucky barrette.

And the Winner Is . . . ?

When I got back to the bench, every-one was huddled around Amanda.

Katie jumped up to give me a hug. "Good job, Dana," she said.

"What's going on?" I asked.

"Amanda lost her barrette," Emily said in a tragic voice.

I looked over at the bench. Hannah Rose had her arm around Amanda. Amanda was staring straight ahead. Her big brown eyes looked bigger than ever.

Coach Jody patted Amanda's shoulder. "Can you remember when you saw it last?" she asked.

Amanda sniffled. "I know I had it on the bars," she said. "And I'm sure I was wearing it when I did my vault. Or maybe I wasn't!" she gasped. "Oh, no! That's why I didn't win!"

I couldn't believe she said that. I wanted to tell her that she didn't win the vault because *I* did. My vault was better than hers. But I kept quiet. No one else said anything either. They were too busy trying to calm Amanda down.

"Don't worry, Amanda," Liz said. "We'll find your barrette." Then she, Emily, and Hannah Rose ran off to look for it.

That left just me and Katie. I knew I should give the barrette back to Amanda. I squeezed it in my hand.

"I have an idea!" Katie cried. "It doesn't have to be your barrette, does it?"

she asked Amanda. "Couldn't something else be lucky?"

"As long as it's lavender," Amanda answered.

Katie reached for her gym bag and dumped it out on the floor. As she began sifting through all her stuff, she muttered, "I must have *something* lavender in here."

Meanwhile, Amanda was getting more and more upset. "What am I going to do?" she cried. "What am I going to do? WHAT-AM-I-GOING-TO-DO?"

I couldn't believe she was making such a fuss about a silly barrette. You would have thought she'd lost her leotard and had to do her routine naked. Everybody else was acting that way, too. No one seemed to care that I didn't feel so hot myself. Except for Katie, no one said a word about *my* beam routine.

I looked at Amanda. I looked at the scoreboard. It still said LEWIS: 9.1 It wasn't a great score. But it wasn't all that bad either. There was always a chance Amanda would mess up and do worse. Anything is possible, I thought.

And that's when I stopped thinking. I tightened my hand around the barrette and went to check out Katie's bag.

She dug through it and pulled out all the first-aid supplies. Then she removed a big tin of talcum powder, a headless Barbie in a pink satin gown, a bunch of those little red paper umbrellas you get in Chinese restaurants, three silver dollars, a yellow-and-blue friendship bracelet, a crumpled photo of her turtle Speedy, two big wooden knitting needles, and a ball of green yarn.

There wasn't one bit of lavender.

"I'm sorry, Amanda," Katie said. "I was sure I had something."

"I'm sorry, too," Coach Jody said. "But I'm afraid you'll have to go on without it, Amanda. I know you think your special colors bring you luck. But you really don't need luck. You have something better than that. Talent!"

Amanda nodded. But she didn't look convinced. She looked scared. Really scared. I almost felt sorry for her.

"Okay, Amanda," Coach Jody said. "We're tied for first in the all-around team competition, and you're the last competitor. All you have to do is get a nine point two and we'll win the cup!"

I gasped. I'd been so busy thinking about the individual medals that I had forgotten about the team competition! But my teammates were all looking at the trophy case in the corner. I could tell that they really, really wanted that shiny silver cup. And so did I.

Math is my worst subject. But even I could figure this one out. If Amanda got a 9.2, she would win the medal and our team would win the cup. If she scored less than that, I would probably win the medal but our team would lose the cup. Of course, there was always a chance she'd get a 9.1 and she and I would be tied. But that way the team would still lose the cup.

I could feel Amanda's barrette digging into my palm. I didn't know what to do.

I didn't want Amanda to win. But I didn't want our team to lose, either.

I looked at Amanda. Her hands were shaking, and she looked as if she was going to cry. Or maybe even faint.

"I can't go up there now," she whispered. "I'll mess up! I'll fall! I can't do it without my lavender barrette."

Suddenly I felt really bad for her. I knew exactly how she felt. Not about her dumb barrette. But about being scared to go on the beam. If Amanda didn't feel safe without her barrette, she probably would mess up! She might even fall off! I didn't want that to happen. Not even to Amanda Calloway.

I ran over to Amanda and held out my hand. "Look, Amanda!" I said. "Here's your barrette. I found it!"

"Oh, my gosh!" Amanda shrieked as I gave her the barrette. "Thank you, Dana. Thank you, thank you, thank you!"

I couldn't believe how happy she looked. I knew I was giving up my chance to beat her, but I felt happy, too.

"Go for it, Amanda," I told her. "You have to win — the whole team is counting on you. *All* of us."

Amanda stared at me for a minute. Then she threw her arms around me. "Thank you," she said. "Now I *can* win!"

Amanda clipped the barrette back in her hair. "Is it straight?" she asked. I giggled and nodded.

The PA system crackled. "Next up,"

said the announcer, "Amanda Calloway, Jody's Gym."

It's weird. When they call out the gymnast's name, they always call out the team she represents. But until now, I'd never really heard it. This time I did.

And I guess I wasn't the only one. Because as I jumped to my feet to cheer Amanda on, so did my teammates. And we stayed there while Amanda marched up to the beam.

I thought I'd seen Amanda's best beam routine. But I hadn't. This one was unreal. She made it look as if the beam were four feet wide instead of just four inches.

It's a good thing we were already standing. Because when the judges held up her score, everyone else jumped up and gave Amanda a standing ovation. A 9.8!

A minute later it was official. Our team had won the silver cup! Amanda won two gold medals and one silver. I won a gold and two silvers. And Katie and Hannah Rose each had a bronze.

After the awards were given out, a photographer from the *Springfield Gazette* asked the whole team to pose for a picture. "You have the gold medals, so you hold the cup," he told Amanda. But she shook her head. "I want Dana to hold the other side," she said. "We *both* won gold medals!"

Katie, Liz, Emily, and Hannah Rose gathered around us. As we all looked at the camera, the photographer said, "Everybody smile."

But he didn't have to tell us that. We were already smiling like crazy.

JUNIOR GYMNASTS

Katie is afraid. Who can help her?

Katie doesn't like to do any backward moves. But now Coach Jody has everyone in the Junior Gymnasts class doing a back walkover on the balance beam! Will Katie have to quit gymnastics? How can she get over her fear?

Junior Gymnasts #2
Katie's Big Move
by Teddy Slater

Backflipping to a bookstore near you.

SCHOLASTIC

JRG1295

Be a Pony Pal!

Anna, Pam, and Lulu want you to join them
on adventures with their favorite ponies!

Order now and you get a free pony portrait bookmark and two
collecting cards in all the books—for you *and* your pony pal!

❏ BBC48583-0	#1 I Want a Pony	$2.99
❏ BBC48584-9	#2 A Pony for Keeps	$2.99
❏ BBC48585-7	#3 A Pony in Trouble	$2.99
❏ BBC48586-5	#4 Give Me Back My Pony	$2.99
❏ BBC25244-5	#5 Pony to the Rescue	$2.99
❏ BBC25245-3	#6 Too Many Ponies	$2.99
❏ BBC54338-5	#7 Runaway Pony	$2.99
❏ BBC54339-3	#8 Good-bye Pony	$2.99
❏ BBC62974-3	#9 The Wild Pony	$2.99
❏ BBC62975-1	#10 Don't Hurt My Pony	$2.99

Available wherever you buy books, or use this order form.

Send orders to Scholastic Inc., P.O. Box 7500, 2931 East McCarty Street,
Jefferson City, MO 65102

Please send me the books I have checked above. I am enclosing $_____ (please add
$2.00 to cover shipping and handling). Send check or money order — no cash or
C.O.D.s please.

Please allow four to six weeks for delivery. Offer good in the U.S.A. only. Sorry,
mail orders are not available to residents in Canada. Prices subject to change.

Name_____Birthdate ___/___/___
     First   Last   M / D / Y

Address_____

City_____State_____Zip_____

Telephone (   )_____ ❏ Boy ❏ Girl

Where did you buy this book? ❏ Bookstore ❏ Book Fair ❏ Book Club ❏ Other

PP1295